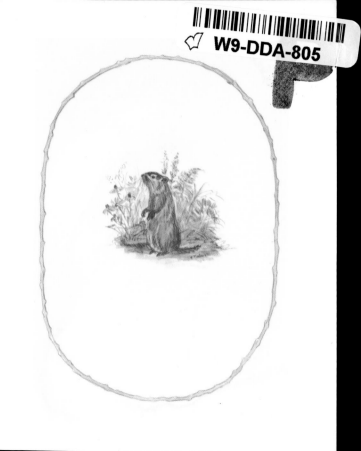

THE LORD IS MY SHEPHERD

The Twenty-Third Psalm

ILLUSTRATED BY
Tasha Tudor

PHILOMEL BOOKS

Special contents copyright © 1980 by Philomel Books,
a division of The Putnam & Grosset Group,
200 Madison Avenue, NY, NY 10016. Miniature
edition published in 1989 by Philomel Books.
Published simultaneously in Canada.
Calligraphy by Jeanyee Wong
Library of Congress number: 79-21734
ISBN 0-399-21892-0
9   10

THE LORD IS
MY SHEPHERD
The Twenty-Third Psalm

The Lord
is my shepherd;

I shall not want.

*He maketh me
to lie down in
green pastures:*

*He leadeth me beside
the still waters.*

He restoreth my soul:
He leadeth me in the
paths of righteousness
for his name's sake.

*Yea, though I walk
through the valley
of the shadow of death,
I will fear
no evil:*

For thou art with me;
thy rod and thy staff
they comfort me.

Thou preparest a table before me in the presence of mine enemies:

*Thou anointest
my head with oil;*

My cup runneth over.

Surely
goodness and mercy
shall follow me
all the days of my life:
and I will dwell
in the house
of the Lord
for ever.

About The Twenty-Third Psalm

The Twenty-Third Psalm is probably the best-known and best-loved of all the one hundred and fifty poems that make up the Book of Psalms, whose Hebrew name is "The Book of Praise." Almost every aspect of our relation to God is the subject of one or another of these works, written more than two thousand years ago. The special sense of serenity and simple trust, and the conviction that the world is in the hands of a loving God have made this psalm, which is one of the group written by King David, particularly appealing. The wording of the King James Version has never been surpassed in the English language, and it is this translation of the Twenty-Third Psalm that Tasha Tudor has chosen for this book.

About Tasha Tudor

Tasha Tudor's illustrations are treasured by people of all ages, and she has won many honors for her books. Born in Boston, she grew up in New England, where she had ample opportunity to observe the beauty of the rural scene and the animals and flowers of the countryside that she depicts with such skill and love in her pencil drawings and delicate watercolors.

Her first book, "Pumpkin Moonshine," a tiny calico-covered volume which she both wrote and illustrated, appeared in 1938. She has illustrated more than 60 books since then, including such classics as *The Wind in the Willows* by Kenneth Grahame, and *Little Women* by Louisa May Alcott, as well as books of her own authorship and anthologies such as the perennially popular *Take Joy!, A Book of Christmas,* and the keepsake *Advent Calendar.* The Twenty-Third Psalm has always been her favorite of the Psalms. She created the larger version, from which this miniature version was created, in 1980.

Ms. Tudor now lives on a farm in Vermont. She is the subject of the biographical portrait, *Drawn from New England: Tasha Tudor,* written by her daughter, Bethany.